Weekly Reader Children's Book Club presents

TROUBLE
AT OTTER CREEK

by Wilma Pitchford Hays

illustrated by Marilyn Miller

Xerox Education Publications

To my great-great-great grandfather, Peter Demo, who settled in the north country (now Vermont) a few years before Ann Story and her five children went to live on their grant near Otter Creek.

Text copyright © 1978 by Wilma Pitchford Hays
Illustrations copyright © 1978 by Xerox Corporation

Publishing, Executive and Editorial Offices:
Xerox Education Publications
Middletown, Connecticut 06457

ISBN 0–88375–214X

Library of Congress Catalogue Card Number:

Weekly Reader Children's Book Club Edition

This book is a presentation of
The Popcorn Bag

Weekly Reader Book Division offers book clubs for children from preschool to young adulthood. All quality hardcover books selected by a distinguished Weekly Reader Selection Board.

For further information write to:
Weekly Reader Book Division
1250 Fairwood Avenue
Columbus, Ohio 43216

Contents

·1·
No Woman Can

Samuel (Sam) Story stopped outside the open front door when he heard his Uncle George's forceful voice. "Ann, you're out of your mind, taking five young 'uns to live on the north grants," his uncle was saying to Mama. "You can't drive off Indians and Yorkers with no man to help you. No *woman* can!"

Sam was afraid again. He had almost made himself believe that Mama could do it. She said they were going north to the new cabin Papa had built last year, before he was killed by a falling tree that he was cutting down. Sam shivered.

A year earlier, 1774, his family had moved from Connecticut to the small town of Rutland in New Hampshire. Eight months ago Papa and fourteen-year old Solomon had gone north through twenty miles of wilderness to land that Papa had bought on Otter Creek. One hundred acres of land that he'd farm as soon as he could clear it of trees, he'd said. Then he'd come back for the rest of the family.

Sam felt again the fear and grief which had come on that late night when he heard his older brother, Solomon, pound on the door of their house in Rutland. As soon as Mama recognized his voice, she had unbolted the door. There Solomon had stood in the candle light, scratched and muddy. His clothes were torn from pushing through twenty miles of wilderness. Sam was afraid the instant he saw that Papa wasn't with him.

Now Papa was dead. Mama had decided that she and the five children must go to the cabin in the wilderness and farm the land Papa had worked so hard to get. Every friend and relative in Rutland was against her plan, but she was going.

Uncle George had come all the way from his own grant near Fort Number Four to talk sense to Mama.

"Ann," he said now, "Amos wouldn't let you go alone to that wilderness if he were here."

"If he were here, I wouldn't have to go alone," she said. "And I'm not alone. I have Solomon and Ephraim and Samuel and Susanna and little Hannah."

"Nothin' but young 'uns," Uncle George said. "Except for Solomon, they're more trouble than help."

Sam went into the house then, anger making him forget his fear. "I'm almost ten," he said, "and I'm not going to be trouble to Mama. There's lots of things I can do to help."

Uncle George put his hand on Sam's shoulder. "Don't get riled, boy," he said. "I know you'll do as much as you can do. But none of you got any idea of what you're up against, living in the wilderness, except maybe Solomon, who's been up there with your papa."

Sam knew what he said was true.

"Has Solomon told you about the Indians who want their land back?" Uncle George asked. "Has he told you about the Yorkers who claim that the boundary of New York is way east into the New Hampshire Grants? You could get up there and find a Yorker family settled on your land — and with just as good a claim to it as you can show."

Sam knew about the land quarrel between the states of New York and New Hampshire. Both claimed the land along their common border. The King of England didn't know much about the new world. He had accidently granted the same land to both states. The governor of each state believed that his state owned the disputed land. Each governor was selling grants to the same land to his own settlers.

"That's why we have to go at once," Mama said. "The land is ours. Amos saved for years and spent all we had for that grant. He worked hard to make a home for us there. If I have to, I can shoot and cut trees and farm as good as anyone," she said. "Once we're on it, I'll never let anyone take our land away from us."

Uncle George looked at her helplessly. "If I could stop you, Ann Story, I would," he said. "A woman and five young 'uns going up there where some men have turned back."

Sam's stomach felt hollow again with doubt. Was everyone else right and Mama wrong?

3

He looked at her. Mama was as tall as Papa and strong. He'd heard Grandma say that Mama was "sure of herself." When she walked, she stepped out like a man.

Sam thought she was pretty and graceful even if she was big. A lady. Blue eyes. Thick, dark red hair in long braids wrapped around her head like a crown. Her hands were large and he'd seen her swing an axe as well as Papa. She was thirty-three, not too old to work hard. Still, he wondered if Uncle George was right. Should they all stay here in Uncle Tracy's house in Rutland and let the relatives help support them?

"The young 'uns need schooling," Uncle George said. "Here they'd have three or four months at the parson's school every winter. Who's going to teach them to read in the wilderness?"

"I will," Mama said. "I'm taking the Bible and a speller. They'll learn to read from that."

"Solomon and Ephraim and I can read already," Sam said, "and figger some."

"They've got to have bread before books," Mama said, "whether we like it or not."

She turned to her packing again. She expected Solomon back with the oxen and ox sled any time. Then they'd go.

Uncle George stood there looking at her. There seemed no way to convince her that a woman could not do what she was planning to do.

Sam said loyally, "If any woman can be a settler in the wilderness, Mama can."

He wished that he was as sure of that as he sounded. Well, they would soon find out.

·2·
Wilderness Home

The first day on the trail wasn't too bad, Sam thought, as he led their one cow on a rope. Everyone walked except for little Hannah. Mama sometimes carried her on her back. Other times she rode on the ox sled piled high with gear—wool blankets, iron kettles, clothing, sugar, flour and such. In the wilderness there would be no store to buy from. They'd have to live on what they could trap, catch, shoot or pick until the corn and pumpkins Papa had planted were grown.

"Maybe that will be a nice way to live," Sam said to Mama, looking back over his shoulder as they walked single-file along the deep rutted trail. "Maybe it will be fun."

She brushed a cloud of mosquitoes away from her face, but smiled. She must have been tired, for she wasted no breath answering.

Susanna, a year younger than Sam, hurried to catch up with Solomon, who led the ox team. She asked him, "Will we see wolves and bears where we live?"

"I hope so," he said. "Nothin' like a wolf or bearskin to keep us warm in winter."

He stopped the oxen with a light touch of his goad on their

noses. "We'll stay here overnight. There's a stretch of spongy swamp ahead. No place to be caught in the dark."

They ate bread, cheese and cooked meat that Mama had brought. They dipped water from a spring to drink, and the cow gave enough milk for Hannah. The cow was going to have a calf in the spring. Then they'd have plenty of milk and a calf to start a herd. Everything looked better to Sam as he rolled up in his blanket to sleep. He pulled a corner of the blanket over his ear. Even in summer a cool breeze came down at night from the mountains, which the early French trappers had named Vert Mont — Green Mountains.

The second morning the deep rutted trail they followed ended in a spruce bog. They walked in water to their ankles. Sam stepped into a deep pool and fell on his knees. He scrambled to his feet, caught the cow's rope again and called to Solomon, "Is this the only way to get to our grant?"

"Except by canoe and portage," Solomon said. "We couldn't take the oxen or much gear the river way. In winter, when this bog freezes over, we can get out easier for supplies."

Solomon was leading the oxen, winding around trees, searching for footing on higher ridges of ground. The sled often stuck. They all had to push and shove from behind while the oxen strained to pull it from the mire.

Mama looked at the mud splattered over her household things but said nothing. Everyone was too tired to talk much. They went around blown down trunks of trees rotting in the water. Jagged points on hidden limbs scratched their legs and bruised their feet.

Live branches brushed across their eyes and pulled off their caps and tore their clothes. As they pushed through the swamp, the woods began to grow dark. Sam realized that the sun was going down. How could they sleep in this muck? They were sopping wet, bitten on face and neck and hands by "No-see-ems." Their needle-like stings went on itching long after the insects were gone.

By the time Solomon halted, it was so dark they all looked like shadows to each other.

"We're through the bog," Solomon said, "but the ground is still too wet to sleep on. We'll have to cut spruce boughs to keep us off the ground."

While Ephraim found patches of grass for the oxen and cows, Sam helped Solomon and Mama cut thick boughs. They piled them about a foot deep for a big bed, where they would all lie down together under blankets.

Ephraim told Mama that the cow did not give any milk. She looked at the water all around them. "None of it's fit to drink," she said. She gave them a little from the jug she had brought for emergency. Then she handed each child a slice of cold cornmeal mush and sausage for supper.

Sam lay on the spruce bed beside his family. Every muscle ached as if he had been beaten with a club. His face burned from insect bites. At the same time he shivered with cold. There was no dry wood for a campfire.

He heard Susanna cough, then sniffle. He didn't know whether she had a cold or was crying. He couldn't blame her if she was.

He wondered again if Mama was right coming here. Was their wilderness land worth all this misery? And when they got there, how would they survive? They sure wouldn't go back to Rutland very often over this trail.

The third day they were so thankful for dry earth under their feet that no one complained. Sam did rub his itching ears often.

Susanna teased him, "If your ears were ordinary size, there wouldn't be so much of them to hurt."

Tired as he was, he grinned. Long ago he had decided that there was nothing he could do about his jug-shaped ears, his freckles and hair redder than Mama's.

"You'd hurt, too," he told her, "if your face wasn't so dirty the bugs can't get through the mud."

By mid-day they came into lighter woods where maple, oak and beech grew. Now and then they reached a small natural break in the forest with patches of grass. One of these breaks was full of bushes loaded with wild blackberries as large as Sam's thumb. They stopped and ate all they could.

They hated to leave this spot where the sun warmed them, but Solomon touched the flanks of the oxen and ordered them to move on.

"We'll reach the cabin before night," he promised. This kept everyone hurrying to keep up with him.

When Sam finally saw the log cabin his father had built in the wilderness, he stopped. They all stopped. Sam didn't look at the others to see if their eyes were filled with tears, but his were wet. It was almost as if Papa was waiting there to welcome them. What

9

he had hoped to give them was waiting, the house and the land.

Everyone began to run at once. They couldn't wait to reach the door.

Solomon shouted behind them, "Wait! Stay back."

The children stopped. Mama came to them with a long gun in her hand. Solomon warned, "Don't ever burst into a strange place until you've looked around. Papa told me — ."

They didn't have time to ask him why. At the sound of his voice, the door of the cabin opened. An Indian came out, knife in hand.

Mama raised her gun. She didn't shoot. She didn't say a word. No one did. They stared at the Indian. He watched them as carefully.

His head was shaved except for a black scalp lock down the center of his skull. He wore buckskin leggings and a red and white checked shirt that came down to his knees — the dirtiest shirt that Sam had ever seen. He had no weapon except the long knife in his hand.

He made no move to use it but began to back away from the door. He edged to the corner of the cabin, and quickly disappeared into the woods behind.

"Mama, why didn't you shoot?" Sam cried.

"Not unless he attacked us first," Mama said.

"With that scalplock, he was a Stockbridge Indian," Solomon said. "They've been friendly. Dressed like he was, he was probably scouting for some settler."

"Maybe a Yorker," Sam said. Uncle George had said they might get here and find that a Yorker had taken over their land.

"Let's see if he stole anything," Solomon said.

Single file, they went into the cabin and looked about cautiously. It was a good, big room. A great stone fireplace for cooking and heating filled the far end. Papa had built two wide bunks for beds, one on each side of the room near the fire. He had split logs and made a table and a couple of benches. That was all the furniture except for a wood box filled with logs for the fireplace.

Solomon looked at the ropes and fishlines hanging on the wall, and at an iron kettle on a hook in the fireplace.

"Nothing's gone that I can see," he said.

"Maybe the Indian only wanted a place to rest," Susanna said.

"Do you think he'll come back?" Sam asked.

"He might," Solomon said. Then he went to the woodbox beside the fireplace. "I'm going to show you something," he said, "in case he does."

Night was coming on. The room was so dark that Sam couldn't see the expression on Solomon's face. But something in his brother's voice made Sam shiver.

"You mustn't ever tell anyone what I'm going to show you," Solomon said. "Papa planned it to save our lives if Indians — or anyone — attacks."

Mama said, "Wait a minute." She took little Hannah into the yard and gave her two pans to bang together. She returned and said, "She's too small to understand what a promise is, but the rest of us know."

Solomon shoved the woodbox away from the wall. He lifted a trap door under it. "This tunnel leads into the root cellar," he said. "The cellar's in the woods back of the cabin. We can escape that way—if we have to—while someone is trying to break down our door."

·3·
Yankees or Yorkers

For several weeks there was scarcely time to do anything but work. The whole family pulled grass and sweet fern and filled bed-ticks that Mama had brought to sleep on. Ephraim, who had a way with animals, herded the oxen and cow to find small patches of clearing where grass grew. Solomon and Mama cut wood for winter fires. "We can't get too much ahead," Solomon warned. "The snow will get so high we can't get into the woods."

Sam's job was to weed and hoe the garden and corn. It wasn't a very large field, but it seemed to grow bigger every day. One noon he stopped for dinner. He looked at his sore hands and tried to straighten his aching back. Inside the cabin door, he dipped water and drank deeply. Then he turned to Mama.

"I'm dizzy from hoeing round and round the stumps in that corn field," he said. "And I'm sick of Solomon bossing me around. He tells me how to do everything as if I didn't have any sense."

Mama looked at him as if she was thinking what to say.

"He's only trying to teach you what Papa taught him," she said.

"He has a lot of responsibility for a boy not yet fifteen. He does it for your own good."

"He doesn't make me feel very good!" Sam said. "The only thing I can do better than Solomon is read and write, and that doesn't count much here."

Mama put a steaming bowl of mashed pumpkin on the table. "I'm getting tired of eating pumpkin and corn mush," she said. "Why don't you go to the creek and catch us a mess of fish for supper?"

Sam felt better at once. He ate quickly. With fishline and hooks over his arm, he stopped at the edge of the woods and turned over damp brown leaves to find fat angle worms for bait.

He whistled as he cut a tree limb for a pole, tied on his line, baited his hook and threw it into the clear deep water of Otter Creek. There, where the water leaped and foamed over a fallen tree, he should catch a trout. He had a strike but jerked too quickly. It felt like a big one. He tried again and again, but caught nothing.

He sat down and leaned his back against a tree trunk. It felt good to sit and look around while he waited for a fish to bite.

Already the leaves of the trees hinted at fall. One limb on a beech had turned a blazing yellow. A maple showed a half dozen scarlet-rimmed leaves among its thick green. Farther into the woods, tall green spruce stood in a dark zig-zag line across the blue sky.

Sam took a comb from his jacket pocket and stretched a piece of oiled paper over it. He began to hum into it and made a fine tune. He had always wanted a fiddle, but a comb and paper were a fair substitute, easier to come by and to carry around.

He was really enjoying himself, making up a cheerful tune. He didn't hear a sound until a hand came down on his shoulder. A big, brown hand. He looked up into the face of the Stockbridge Indian who had come from their cabin a month ago.

Sam threw himself forward onto the ground and tried to roll into the creek. He could swim. Maybe he'd escape.

The Indian caught him. At the same instant a fish struck his line. Sam saw the pole moving along the ground, being pulled into the creek. He yelled. The Indian grabbed the pole with one hand but held onto Sam's leg with the other.

Sam didn't know that Indians smiled, but this one did as he lifted a trout almost two feet long from the water. Then he frowned at Sam and pointed at the boiling current.

"Wunageequtuc cold, fast," he said. "You die."

Sam thought he meant to kill him. Then he realized the Indian was only warning him of the danger of the creek. Wunageequtuc must be the Indian name for Otter Creek.

The Indian killed the trout with a quick blow to the head. He took the boy by the arm and led him through the woods to a man hacking underbrush with a hatchet.

He was a white man, although his skin was weathered brown. He wore buckskin leggins and a hunting shirt and a plaid peaked cap on the back of his head. Sam wondered why he was cutting a

15

path, only body wide, through thick underbrush when he could walk a little way and follow a creek bank with no trouble at all. And he was cutting on Papa's land.

"We heard your music," the man said. "Just wanted to ask you a few questions. Are you one of the Amos Story family?"

"Yes," Sam said as polite as possible for the way he felt. He didn't know what this man would do.

"Didn't mean for Hunk—he's my helper—to scare you," the man said, nodding toward the Indian. "My name's McKay. Dan McKay."

A Scot, John thought, and looked again at the plaid bonnet the man wore.

"Was your father a Green Mountain man?" Dan McKay asked.

"I don't know," Sam said.

He knew that Green Mountain men were the New Hampshire Yankees who had banded together to keep the settlers from New York from taking their grants away from them.

"Is your brother a Green Mountain man?" McKay asked.

"No," Sam answered quickly. "Solomon's not old enough to join fighting men."

The man spat. "That Ethan Allen would enlist his own grand-mother to keep this land for New Hampshire," he said.

Then Sam knew. "You're a Yorker," he cried.

"Not exactly," McKay said. "I work for a Yorker. I'm surveying this land for a New York settler who paid for it, fair and square. He's got papers to prove it. And when I finish marking this line, he'll move in."

17

"But Papa settled this land first," Sam said. "It's ours. We've got papers, too. We're not looking for trouble, but we're going to live here, no matter what. Mama says so."

Dan McKay lifted his hatchet as if this was the end of what he had to say. "You tell your brother that he'll get some of that trouble you ain't looking for if he joins up with that big moose, Ethan Allen."

The Indian handed the trout to Sam. He took it and ran home.

The family sat around the supper table, eating broiled trout and talking about what Sam had learned from the surveyor McKay.

Solomon said, "Papa said Ethan Allen is hot-headed and likes a fight. He's done some terrible things to New Yorkers who tried to keep land this side of the river. He's burned houses and run them out, even men with families. But if it wasn't for him and the other Green Mountain men, we wouldn't have a chance to hold onto our grants."

Sam looked at Mama's face, lighted by flames in the fireplace. Finally she said, "Ethan Allen may not always be right. But we have no choice except to ask him to help us. Do you know where to reach him, Solomon?"

"Papa knew where he lived," Solomon answered. "It must be in his papers."

"Sam," Mama said. "I'll clear the table. You get the writing paper. Write Ethan Allen a letter. Tell him that a Yorker threatens to settle on land that is ours. Tell him we're going to stay."

"How are we going to get the letter to him?" Sam asked. There were no neighbors or towns nearby.

"Get it written," she said. "We'll send it by the first trapper or woodsman that passes by."

The next day Sam brought her the letter. He said, "No one's been here in more than a month. Maybe no one will come by before winter. But I've got an idea. I think McKay would take it to town for us when he finishes surveying. He wasn't mean to me, just gruff. I'll ask him."

"He'd never carry a letter to be delivered to Ethan Allen," Solomon said.

"I wouldn't tell him who it was for," Sam said.

Mama looked thoughtful. "Maybe Sam's right," she said, "That letter must be mailed. The surveyor would carry one addressed to Uncle George. I'll put Ethan Allen's letter inside it. George will get it to him."

When Sam took the letter to him, the Scot looked a little puzzled yet pleased, too.

"Glad to oblige," he said. "You're just in time, too. We're leaving tomorrow. No hard feelings, boy. As I see it, both you folks and the Yorker I'm working for have the same right to claim this land. It's just too bad. It's a mixup I wouldn't want to be in."

·4·
Green Mountain Men

Sam was picking the last wild purple asters of fall when he thought he heard footsteps in the woods. "Hey! Who is it?"

No one answered. He listened and listened but heard nothing

more. If it had been a Green Mountain man, he'd answer. Probably some animal.

Sam took the flowers to Mama. "It's been two weeks since we sent the letter by McKay," he said. "Do you think Ethan Allen got it? Do you think he will come?"

"We'll just have to wait and see," she said.

For days Solomon and Mama and Sam split logs and built a lean-to shelter on a back corner of the cabin for the cow. Beside the shelter they piled a wall of wild pasture hay that Ephraim foraged. The animals couldn't get grass for themselves after snows were deep.

"The oxen can stand the cold if they keep close to the cabin out of the wind," Solomon said. "They won't go far from this feed."

One evening in November when the moon was full, touching the tops of the pine trees with silver, Sam thought he heard men moving around outside. He ran and looked through a gun hole in the split log shutters over a window. He saw only bare yard, some tangled withered weeds, and leaves rattling down from trees.

"Sam, go back to bed," Susanna said.

"I thought it might be Green Mountain men," he answered.

"More likely the cow stamping her feet," Solomon said. As usual he was right. Sam thought Ethan Allen was a long time answering his letter.

Winter winds came with pelting snow. Drifts piled up around the cabin higher than the windows. The family spent hours each day cutting wood to keep the big fireplace going night and day.

When the spring of water froze over, they melted snow in a big iron kettle.

It was a struggle to get through the snow to the root cellar once a week and bring back pumpkin and salt-meat. When Sam reached down into the salt-brine for meat, he felt a strange excitement, knowing that the open end of the tunnel was hidden back of the salt barrels. The tunnel led from the house and was barely large enough for a big man to crawl through. Sam had never entered it. No use getting into a black dirt burrow like that unless he had to.

When their work was done each day, the family sat close to the fire and took turns reading the Bible aloud. Mama called out numbers for them. They added in their heads to see who could get the sum first. They spelled aloud, too. They sang all the old songs they could remember. Sam made up some cheery tunes to play on his comb. They didn't need sad music to remind them of troubles.

At last Sam waked one morning and knew the cold wasn't creeping through the cabin as it had on other mornings when the fire was low. He jumped out of bed and ran to open the door. A thawing wind had worked all night. He could see brown earth between patches of white. Mist rolled up from the swamp below Otter Creek. He smelled the fog and damp wood thawing.

"Mama," he cried. "Spring's come."

Everyone piled out of bed, smiling and laughing. Solomon said, "We can start planting before long."

This sobered Sam. Maybe the Yorker settler would come soon

to get his crops planted on time. There hadn't been a word from Ethan Allen. How could they stop the Yorker alone?

A few days later the cow had twin calves. She began to give enough milk for her family and theirs. Solomon showed them how to gather blobs of spruce sap where it sometimes formed on the tree trunk as the sap rose in the spring. Even Mama chewed spruce gum, enjoying its fresh woods taste. As the snow melted they found and nibbled wintergreen leaves.

"I never thought I'd get so hungry for anything green," Susanna said.

"It won't be long until we can gather a pot of poke greens and fiddleheads," Mama said.

Sam and Susanna were in the woods gathering the first tender furls of fiddlehead ferns when they heard men talking. "No way of knowing who they are," Susanna whispered.

"We better warn Mama," Sam said. They ran to the cabin ahead of the men. "Someone's coming. Maybe it's Green Mountain men."

"Or Yorkers," Mama said. "Close the door. Don't open it until we know which."

During the day they always removed the split-log guards from across the windows. Now all the family gathered to watch four men come from the woods. Three men were ordinary size, not much taller than Mama. Their leader was the biggest man that Sam had ever seen. He wore a red stocking cap turned back in a band above his heavy dark eyebrows. His deerskin jacket was fringed at bottom and down the length of his sleeves.

"He looks like a giant," Susanna whispered.

"He has to be Ethan Allen" Sam said.

"Hall-ooo in there," the big man called. He stopped and waited
or an answer as if he had learned not to approach a strange cabin
without announcing himself.

Mama went to the door, everyone else close behind her. "Yes?"
he asked, opening it a little.

"Ma'm," he asked, "You Mrs. Story? We're Green Mountain
men come to see how you're gettin' along."

"Did you get my letter?" Sam called.

"That's why we're here," Ethan Allen said.

Mama opened the door wide. "Come right in," she said.

He introduced the men. "My younger brother, Levi. My cousin,
eth Warner. And yonder's Tom Rowley, the singingest man in
hese parts. Folks call him 'Minstrel of the Green Mountains'."

Mama said, "I'm cooking supper. You must stay the night."

Sam turned to Tom Rowley. "I can play a comb," he said, "but
wish I had a fiddle."

"I wish I had my fiddle with me," Tom said, "but we can make
ome pretty good music without it."

They ate supper together, then sat before the fireplace to sing and
alk. Everyone knew the old hymns and Tom Rowley taught them
ongs he'd made up. Sam liked the one about chasing Yorkers:

> *Yorkers on the run-run-run,*
> *From Green Mountain men,*
> *Run. Run. Run. Run. Run!*

Little Hannah fell asleep on Mama's lap and she put her to bed.
Susanna was so sleepy, she went, too. The three boys stayed up to
hear what the men had to say.

"You're getting some neighbors up in this north country,"
Ethan Allen told them. "Man's building a cabin across the swamp.
Going to bring his family up from Connecticut."

"Papa came from Norwich, Connecticut," Sam said.

Mama said, "What's troubling us is the 'neighbor' that claims
our own land. What can we do about the Yorker, short of standing
him off with a long gun?"

"We've sent a lot of Yorkers packing in the last five years," Ethan

said. "Enough to put a price on my head. New York offers twenty pounds in gold to bring me in — for jail or dead."

"We just drove some Yorkers off our own grants on the Onion River," Seth Warner said. "They chased us all day yesterday, but I think we lost them."

Sam thought they didn't seem too worried about angry Yorkers with guns hunting them.

"Ma'm," Ethan Allen said, "I don't aim to discourage you, but we've got more than Yorkers to worry us now. The thirteen colonies are really heated up over the British sending armies to Boston to collect taxes. We're liable to be at war — a revolution. If it comes to fightin', no settler will be safe up here so close to Canada."

"Us Yankees were Britishers first," Mama said. "I don't believe British soldiers will kill women and children. We'll stay unless they burn us out."

Ethan Allen smiled. "I heard you had spunk, Ann Story," he said, "and we've got some plans. We're trying to hold a meeting of the settlers on the grants — to vote this north country free of New Hampshire. We even got a name for the new territory if we do break away by ourselves. Vermont. What do you think of that?"

"From Vert Mont," Sam said. "Green Mountains. Would we be the fourteenth colony?"

"That's moving pretty fast," Ethan Allen said. "But we'd be a free and independent territory. We wouldn't have to fight the British if we decided not to join the colonies."

Sam didn't think Seth Warner liked the sound of that, for Seth frowned. "We wouldn't have the protection of those thirteen colonies either," he said.

"Nothin's settled yet," Ethan Allen said.

It was time to go to bed. The four men rolled up in blankets on the floor. Sam, lying on the boys' bed between Solomon and Ephraim, heard the visitors snoring peacefully. He was too excited to sleep. He tried to sort out what Ethan Allen had told them.

The Yorker settlers from the Colony of New York had always been a real threat to New Hampshire settlers like his own family. Now the British soldiers, stationed just over the river at Crown Point, soon could be enemies, too. And North Country Yankees

26

like his family were thinking of pulling away from New Hampshire to become the free territory of Vermont.

Sam didn't know what he thought about all this news. It was too much to digest at one time.

·5·
Capture

Sam waked and slipped past the sleeping men to the door. He opened it a crack and peeked out. There was a pink streak of light in the eastern sky. Behind him everyone began to stir as if they smelled the fresh air he'd let into the cabin.

As he started to close the door, he thought he saw the glint of sun on metal. He watched a second, then turned to the men.

"Someone's out there in the pines," he said.

Quickly the four men were out of their blankets with long guns in hand.

Solomon said, "Maybe the cow again."

The cow was allowed to roam with her twin calves, for she never went far from the cabin. Sam shook his head. "I saw the sun reflect on a gun barrel."

He went to the window as fast as the Green Mountain men. The cabin was surrounded by men in buckskins and with long guns.

"Yorkers," Seth said. "They followed our trail."

"Ma'm," Ethan Allen said. "We don't want them to shoot at this

cabin with you and the young'uns in it. If someone will open that
door, we'll make a run for the woods."

"No," Mama said. "There's a dozen of them. They'll shoot you
sure."

Solomon knew what she was thinking. He ran and pulled the
woodbox away from the wall. He lifted the trap door. "Down
here," he said, "The tunnel comes out in the root cellar in the
woods. They can't see you from here."

They didn't need to be told twice. Ethan Allen let the others go
first. Then he ducked into the dark burrow. Sam thought his
shoulders might be too wide for the tunnel, but he crawled away.

Solomon scarcely had time to push the woodbox back when the Yorkers began to pound on the cabin door. Quickly the children picked up the men's blankets from the floor and threw them on the two beds.

"Open up," A Yorker shouted. "Surrender or we'll shoot."

Mama opened the door wide and stepped out of the cabin. "Surrender? Who?" she asked.

The leading Yorker looked suprised, as if he hadn't expected a woman—a woman with five stairsteps of children looking out from the doorway behind her.

"Ma'm," he said. "We traced Ethan Allen to this cabin, and

we're going to take him. He's been raiding Yorker farms on the Grants for too long. Burning cabins and crops. Running off our livestock. Threatening men so they give up what's theirs."

Mama said, "Sounds like he's a terrible man."

The leader blinked. "He is, Ma'm. I'm sorry, but we must search your cabin."

"You're welcome to," Mama said.

With their long guns ready, the men entered the cabin one by one. Sam saw the disappointment on their faces when they saw there was no one here but a woman and children.

"Won't you have some tea and corn mush?" Mama asked. "Won't take a minute. I always keep water boiling in the kettle."

"Thank you," the leader said. "We haven't eaten since yesterday."

The Yorkers leaned their long guns against the wall and sat down at the table. Sam knew Mama was trying to give the Yankee men time to get away from the root cellar.

She was making tea at the fireplace when the door opened and the four Green Mountain men burst into the cabin with long guns pointed. The Yorkers didn't have time to do a thing but sit there gaping. Ethan Allen's men had gone through the tunnel and back to the house too fast.

Now Sam saw why the Yorkers hated and feared Ethan Allen.

"I'm giving you Yorkers one more chance," the big man roared, and shoved a gun into the leader's chest. "Get off the grants. Stay off. If I ever catch you, or any other Yorker, this side of the river again, I'll shoot you without warning."

Seth, Levi and Tom gathered up the Yorkers' guns. Ethan Allen nodded toward the door. "Now get," he said to the twelve unarmed Yorkers. "If you want to live, stay in New York. These grants are Yankee land. You just remember that."

The Yorkers left, followed by the Green Mountain men.

"Mama," Sam said. "I don't think that Yorker will come here to settle on our land now. Do you?"

"It isn't likely," Mama said. "Still, no one gives up land easily."

·6·
Burned Out

All day after Ethan Allen's men took the Yorkers away, Mama worked. She kneaded bread and baked beans. Once in awhile she stopped and looked around the cabin.

"Are you worried that they'll come back?" Sam asked her.

"What will we do?" Susanna asked. Sam knew his sister was brave for a nine-year old, but anyone with sense would be worried.

Suddenly Mama smiled as if she had made up her mind. "We're going on a picnic to Otter Creek tomorrow," she said.

Solomon looked at her in surprise. "I've brought in the oxen to turn over the stump field for planting corn," he said.

"You do that," Mama said, "and Ephraim can look after the cows. The rest of us will picnic."

Sam could scarcely believe that Mama had forgotten the Yorkers' threat so soon. Hannah raced for their fishlines. "I like trout," the little girl said.

"Mama," Susanna said. "You're planning something more than a picnic. I know."

"Yes," Mama said. "We're going to hunt for a cave in those bluffs along the creek. We must be prepared. If we ever have to escape through the tunnel, we'll have a place to go."

The children looked at her. Sam wondered if his sisters' and brothers' hearts were beating as hard as his.

Morning came sunny and warm. They could hardly wait to get started with their loaf of bread and baked beans. Mama said, "Sam, bring a spade. Susanna carry the hatchet. We'll need to dig and cut down brush when we find the right place."

It was so much fun trooping through the woods, exploring along the creek, stopping to eat and fish, that Sam forgot they were looking for a place to hide if enemies came. He was helping Hannah pull in a fish that was too big for her when Susanna called. "I found a hiding place. Come see!"

Everyone followed her along the creek bank to an outcrop of earth and rock. "It's not a big cave," she said, "but I think we could all get in."

Mama stopped under the jutting roof and looked into the dimly lighted place. "You children can stand up in it, but I'll have to bend over," she said. "It's almost as deep and wide as our cabin. We'll dig out enough dirt to level the floor. And bring pine boughs in case the earth stays damp."

"Did you notice," Susanna asked, proud that she had found it, "that the brush is thick in front of the opening? As soon as the bushes leaf out, no one will ever know we are living in the cave."

The next few weeks they spent all their spare time making the cave livable. Mama cut planks and piled them against a wall to make a shelf. She stored some blankets there, a spade and hatchet, a hammer, two kettles, and anything she could spare from regular use in the cabin. It was a good thing she did.

They had lived in the cabin just one year. The new crop of corn was high, green peas and beans in the garden. Solomon left the cabin early one morning to hunt rabbits for stew. He returned before the rest of the family were fully dressed. Sam said, "You weren't gone long enough to get anything."

"Long enough to see trouble," Sam said. "There's a band of Mohawks coming this way. They camped last night on Otter Creek. They don't seem in a hurry. They aren't even quiet. I watched them awhile from the trees."

"Maybe they're only passing by," Susanna said hopefully.

"Mohawks are New York Indians," Solomon said. "They've no good reason to be over here on New Hampshire Grants."

He looked at Mama. "There's too many of them to hold off with our two long guns."

She went to the mantel, took flint to build fires and put it in her pocket. "Bundle up extra clothes," she said. "Each of you take your own." She was already making up a pack of flour, beans, salt and other supplies.

"They may be friendly and pass by," she said. "We can't be sure of that."

"We'd meet them if we go to the cave," Solomon said.

"We'll hide at the edge of the swamp," Mama said. "Ephraim, drive the cow and calves and oxen into the woods or the Indians will take them. We can hunt them later."

"I'll take them deep into the woods and stay with them," he said and hurried away.

Everyone moved so fast that Sam scarcely had time to be afraid until they started for the woods that edged the swamp. Loaded with bundles, they couldn't move quickly. The back of his neck tingled when he thought about arrows speeding after them, or bullets if the Mohawks owned guns.

They stopped far enough into the swamp to be hidden but close enough to watch the cabin. The ground under them was so spongy they rested their bundles on their feet to keep the supplies dry.

"That many Indians don't have to be careful," Mama said, "so they aren't likely to choose a path through the swamp. I think we'll be safe here until it's dark enough to go to the cave."

They didn't have long to wait. The Mohawks ran from the woods and rushed the cabin. Their cries sent chills down Sam's spine. They swarmed into his home until it could hold no more. In minutes they came out the doorway again, holding high the things they were carrying away.

"Our goose down pillows," Susanna cried.

"Grandpa's clock!" Solomon said.

Sam said, "We have two guns they didn't get and cooking kettles and blankets."

Mama said, "Pray God they won't hunt for us!"

Sam swallowed in terror as he saw two Indians light pine torches from a kettle of live coals another Indian carried. Indians brought pine boughs and stacked them around the cabin.

The Mohawks touched the pine with fire. Flames leaped up all around the cabin. Not one of the family could speak as they watched the heavy plank walls smoulder, catch fire, blaze and crumble. At last the roof fell into flames.

Sam couldn't keep tears from his eyes. All that Papa had built, the cabin, beds, table and benches, was gone.

Clouds of smoke blurred their vision now. Red and black cinders fell on them and set their clothing afire. They slapped each other to put out the flames. When the great fire died down to a pile of coals, they could see again. The Indians were gone.

"Do you think Yorkers sent them to burn us out?" Sam asked Mama.

"I don't know," she said. "They could want this land themselves."

"It may have been their hunting ground, before we came," Sam said.

"I do know," Mama said, "that we've got a cave to live in until we can build another cabin."

Sam wasn't sure he had heard right. "We're going to build a cabin? We don't know *how*."

"Solomon helped Papa," she said. "He can tell us what we need to know."

It was night before they dared leave the swamp to go to the cave. It wasn't safe to build a fire. They ate bread for supper and went to bed.

Sam, wrapped in a blanket on pine boughs, watched through the wide mouth of the cave. Fireflies flashed their lights off and on far into the night. He turned and twisted, trying to sleep.

This cave wasn't a place he'd choose to live in, but they were lucky to have it now. He heard Mama turning restlessly, too. Maybe it wasn't so much luck as it was Mama's planning ahead that saved them. He thought of Uncle George's urging her not to take the children into the north country to live. If he could see them now, he'd be sure he was right.

·7·
A Woman Can

At dawn the family returned to the cabin site. They found a great pile of wood ashes that the wind was carrying away.

"The fireplace is still standing," Sam called.

"That saves time and work," Mama said.

The cow and her calves stood at the edge of the clearing as if they were uncertain that this was the place where they belonged. Ephraim was with them and called, "I'm glad you're all right."

Mama said, "I didn't think to bring a kettle so you could milk the cow. Susanna, run back to the cave and get one. You'll have to empty the dried beans on a blanket."

As they ate their breakfast of bread and milk, Sam saw that Mama's mind was wholly on rebuilding their home. She had planned jobs for each child, even Hannah.

"After we cut a log" she said to the little girl, "you gather the chips of bark and make a pile of kindling right here. It will be close to the door when our cabin's up."

Hannah was glad to help and ran around picking up sticks and even dried leaves for her "wood pile."

Ephraim would go on doing the milking and herding the cow and calves and oxen. "And Ephraim," Mama said, "we'll need new wooden trenchers and spoons. You'll have time to carve them while you're looking after the animals."

Mama was the only one strong enough to help Solomon fell trees with an axe, so Susanna was to cook and wash their clothes. "Our wash tub burned," Susanna said, "and we don't have an oven."

"Dip the clothes up and down in the creek," Mama said, "and dry them on the grass. I've heard that Indians bake corn cakes on hot stones. You'll manage until we repair the fireplace oven."

"If Indians can, I can," Susanna said.

But the first cakes she baked were burned on the outside and soggy inside. The beans were scorched, too. Sam tasted his and spit them on the ground. Susanna's eyes filled with tears. Everyone was hungry after a long day's work, and no one wanted to eat what she had cooked.

"I wasn't too good a cook when I began," Mama said. "Burn the cook fire down until you have lots of hot coals. But don't let it flame around the kettle — that's what burns it."

They worked every day, rain or shine, and returned to the cave to sleep. Sam kept the fields and garden hoed and weeded. His back often ached and his hands were sore, but the work didn't seem such a burden now. He was responsible and his older brother no longer had to tell him how to do it.

Day after day Sam heard the trees fall as Mama and Solomon swung their axes in the woods nearby. When his own work was done, Sam often helped hunt for trees as nearly the same size as possible.

"Logs of the same size fit together better," Solomon told him. "Papa was particular about the trees we cut."

He showed Sam how to trim the limbs from the fallen trees with a hatchet to make straight, long logs. Then they cut and smoothed the top and bottom of each log to make it flat.

"They'll lay on top of each other without rolling if they are flattened," Solomon explained.

Carefully Mama and Solomon notched grooves in the ends of the logs so they could be fitted together and hold tight.

After three weeks they had prepared enough logs for the cabin. With a chain, Solomon hitched each log to an oxen and dragged it from the woods to the cabin site. Sam's back ached just to look at the great piles of logs waiting to be made into four walls and a roof.

"Can the oxen help you build?" he asked.

"They can pull right up to the chimney," Mama said, "and Solomon is making a winch to help them lift part-way. But they can't lay one log on top of another and fit it. Solomon and I have to do that."

Sam wanted so much to help, but he wasn't big enough to do what they had to do. The night before the raising of the walls began, Sam was worried. Mama and Solomon were used to hard work and they were strong. Still, Mama was a woman and his brother was not full grown. What if they couldn't lift the logs up as the walls grew higher?

He felt better the next morning when the bottom row of logs was fitted with no trouble. With the back of his hatchet Sam drove in wooden pegs the family had whittled to secure the joints. He shoved hard against each joint and was pleased to find them tight.

By the end of the third day, one wall was as high as Mama's shoulder. Now the work was very difficult. Both Mama and Solomon's faces were red with strain. Their hands and arms bled where the rough bark scratched them. They staggered under the weight of a log they were trying to lift above their heads. Sam ran to help them.

"Get back," Mama called, so angry that Sam stopped and swallowed hard. He only wanted to help.

At last the log was in place. Mama turned to him. "Getting too close is a good way to be killed or hurt," she said. She sank down on a log to rest.

She looked so tired that Sam ran and brought her a drink of water. She took the gourd dipper and smiled. Sam knew then that Mama wasn't really angry with him. She just didn't want him hurt if the log accidently slipped and fell.

Two weeks later the four walls were up; the stone fireplace again filled the back. They cut a window on two sides and a door in front.

"Now that the logs are laid, we have to chink them," Solomon said. "Sam and Susanna can both help with that." He showed them how to mix clay and pounded dry leaves with water to make a thick mud paste.

"Like mud pies," little Hannah said and squished the dough through her fingers.

Carefully they pushed the mud into the cracks between the logs, filling every tiny vein of light. Sam saw that Susanna was good at chinking.

"How can you dab the mud in so fast and so neat?" he asked.

She looked at the globs of mud he had smeared over the logs. "Smooth it carefully with the back side of your hand," she said and showed him.

When he still had trouble, she found a wood chip to push the mud in and smooth it to dry. Sam tried this trick and found it worked for him, too.

The afternoon that they finished the cabin, they all sat down to look at it. Mama was still full of plans. "As soon as we build a table and benches," she said to Solomon, "you and Ephraim can take the ox sled and go into town for supplies."

"As soon as the swamp freezes over," he said.

"While you're gone," she planned, "Sam and I can build a shelter for the cows and maybe a coop for a few chickens. You could bring back a dozen hens and a rooster."

"We'd have eggs to cook with," Susanna cried.

"And eggs to set in the spring," Mama said. "We'll raise a flock of chickens."

Sam couldn't take his eyes off the new cabin he had helped to build. It looked every bit as strong as the one Papa had built. He looked beyond the cabin at the corn growing high around rotting tree stumps. Nearly every stalk had two or more ears on it. They'd have cornmeal to last all year. The pumpkins were turning orange and too big for him to reach around. They had raised and dried a bushel of shell beans.

"I wish Uncle George could see us now," Sam said. "He'd know a woman *can* be a settler."

Mama smiled. "A woman can with children like mine," she said.

Sam smiled at her, too. He knew they all had a right to be proud.

Afterword

This book is based on the true experiences of Ann Story and her five children, who settled near the town of Salisbury in 1775 when Vermont was still a part of the New Hampshire Grants. A small depression on the bank of Otter Creek, where their cave used to be, can still be seen today.

Even after the Revolutionary War began, and settlers were urged to return to their original homes in Connecticut or to go for safety to the towns, the Story family lived in the cabin they built after the Indians had burned them out. As the children grew older, the family did go to Rutland to spend the winters and the children could attend school three or four months of each year.

W.P.H.